Øx 10/11

# BUN BUN'S BIRTHDAY

Richard Scrimger • Illustrated by Gillian Johnson

Tundra Books

Text copyright © 2001 by Richard Scrimger
Illustrations copyright © 2001 by Gillian Johnson

Published in Canada by Tundra Books, *McClelland & Stewart Young Readers*,
481 University Avenue, Toronto, Ontario M5G 2E9

Published in the United States by Tundra Books of Northern New York,
P.O. Box 1030, Plattsburgh, New York 12901

Library of Congress Control Number: 00-135454

**Canadian Cataloguing in Publication Data**

Scrimger, Richard, 1957-
    Bun Bun's birthday

ISBN 0-88776-520-3

I. Johnson, Gillian.    II. Title.

PS8587.C745B86 2001     jC813'.54     C00-932279-5
PZ7.S64Bu 2001

We acknowledge the support of the Canada Council for the Arts and the Ontario
Arts Council for our publishing program.

We acknowledge the financial support of the Government of Canada through the
Book Publishing Industry Development Program for our publishing activities.

Design: K.T. Njo

Printed in Hong Kong, China

1 2 3 4 5 6        06 05 04 03 02 01

*For Thea, Imogen, Ed, and my other son,*
*who wishes to be nameless.*

R.S.

———

*For Katy*

G.J.

**Sproing, Sproing, Sproing.** Winifred and Eugene were bouncing on the big bed in their parents' room. From the top of her bounce, Winifred could twirl and even see the street below. Eugene was not such a good bouncer. Sometimes he sproinged, and sometimes he thumped.

Winifred bounced onto her bottom, then back onto her feet. Eugene jumped extra hard and landed on the floor.

Sproing. Thump. "Ow!"

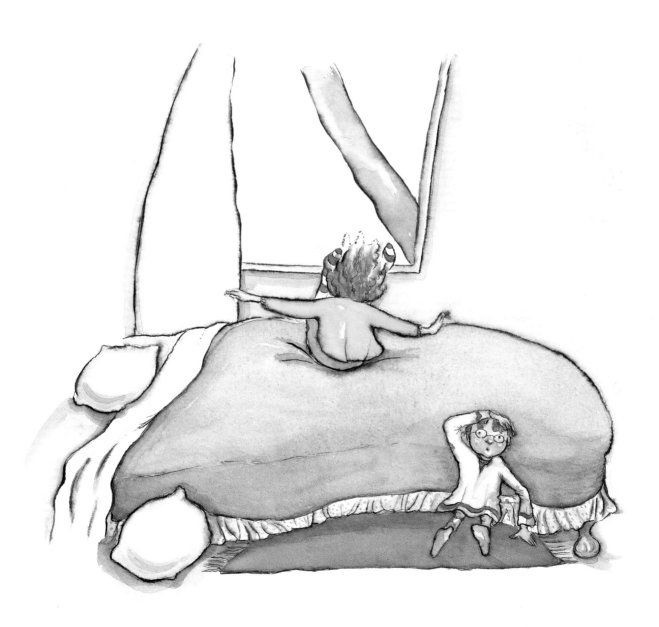

"What are you two doing up there?" called Daddy.
"Nothing," said Winifred and Eugene together.

"Better stop it," called Daddy.
Just then there was a loud BANG, and Bun Bun shrieked from downstairs.

The living room looked like a magical kingdom. There were colored streamers and balloons. A banner with letters hung in the doorway. Winifred couldn't read yet, but she knew her letters. The banner didn't spell her name.

Bun Bun's real name was Brenda, but nobody called her that. She was sitting on the floor, crying.

Daddy was standing on a chair, holding a balloon. He reached up high.

"See, Bun Bun!" Winifred said, holding her up. "It's a party! Hooray!"

The chair wobbled. The balloon burst – **BANG**. Bun Bun shrieked again. Daddy sighed.

Mommy came in, along with a lot of cold air. "Want to see the cake I bought?" she said.

Winifred put Bun Bun down and ran into the kitchen.

The cake had yellow icing and little
pink roses, and writing. There was a teddy
bear in the center. It was a beautiful cake.

"What does the writing say?" asked Winifred.

"It says, 'Happy Birthday, Bun Bun,'" said Mommy.

"Bun Bun?" said Winifred.

"It's her very first birthday today," said Mommy. "She is one year old."

"Bun Bun? This cake is for Bun Bun?" Winifred frowned. "The decorations are for Bun Bun? The party is for Bun Bun?"

"That's right," said Mommy gaily. "Everything for Bun Bun."

Winifred ran from the room.

"What are you doing in here?" asked Eugene.

The upstairs hall closet was the biggest one in the house. Winifred was sitting on the floor at the back of the closet, beside her mother's summer clothes.

"I'm hiding. What are **you** doing here?"

"I'm looking for the tape. Daddy needs it to hang up more balloons."

"Balloons, hah!" said Winifred. She moved her foot. "I can't see any tape," she said.

"Okeydokey," said Eugene.

"You know who the balloons are for, don't you?" said Winifred. "Not for you. Not for me. They're for Bun Bun. Everything is for Bun Bun."

"It's a party," said Eugene. "Nana is coming. And Uncle Dave. And Keisha and her mom from down the street. I can hardly wait!"

"But it's not Bun Bun's turn for a birthday," said Winifred, with sudden tears in her eyes. "It's **my** turn. My birthday comes next after yours, and it was your turn last."

"I got a cement truck," said Eugene. "And building blocks. Remember? The cake had chocolate icing."

"That's why I'm hiding," said Winifred. "Mommy and Daddy will never find me here."

Eugene frowned. "They'll never find you anywhere else," he said. Eugene had an odd way of thinking about things.

"I'm going to hide here until after the party," said Winifred.

"Can I have your piece of cake?" asked Eugene.

"Go away, Eugene."

"Okeydokey." He left.

Winifred moved her foot off the tape.

"Winifred, where are you?" called Mommy.

Winifred smiled to herself.

"Winifred, come out. Are you hiding under the bed, darling? Oh, please come out."

She sounded so worried that Winifred's heart melted inside her, like a popsicle on a hot day. She forgave her mother. She opened the closet door and went to the front bedroom. After the dark closet, the sunlight hurt her eyes.

"Of course I'm not hiding under the bed, Mommy," she said. "That would be dangerous. If someone was jumping on the bed, I might get hurt."

"But who would be jumping on the bed?" Mommy asked.

"I found the tape," said Winifred. "I think Daddy is looking for it."

Mommy smiled. Winifred was glad she had come out of hiding.

Mommy put her arm around Winifred and spoke gently near her ear.

"You know, dear, **you** had a party on your first birthday."

"I did?" said Winifred.

Mommy and Winifred sat together on the bed.

"Oh, yes. We were living in an apartment building then – you and Daddy and me – and we invited everyone from our floor."

"Why don't I remember?" said Winifred.

"Because you were only one year old. No one remembers their first birthday."

Winifred clasped her hands tightly. She tried to understand. "So, I will remember Bun Bun's first birthday, but she won't. Is that right?"

"Yes," said Mommy.

"So, it is really my party today, more than Bun Bun's. Is that right?"

"Well . . . ," said Mommy.

"When Bun Bun is older, I will tell her about today. All that I remember. All that she missed."

"I'm sure she will like that," said Mommy.

A snowball exploded against the front window. That could mean only one thing. Winifred, Eugene, and Bun Bun looked out. A funny frog figure in a big overcoat and a hat like a flowerpot was bending down to scrape more snow into a snowball.

"Nana's here!" Winifred cried, waving vigorously.

"Then we're ready to start the party," said Mommy.

"And my birthday is next. Right?" asked Winifred.